DINO-BOARDING

LISA WHEELER

ILLUSTRATIONS BY
BARRY GOTT

 CAROLRHODA BOOKS · MINNEAPOLIS

To Andreas Haroulakis and his
surfboard, Paul Verrette and
his skateboard, and Andrew
Karre and his snowboard. —L.W.

For Rose, Finn, and Nandi —B.G.

Carolrhoda Books
A division of Lerner Publishing Group, Inc.
241 First Avenue North
Minneapolis, MN 55401 USA

For reading levels and more information, look up this title at www.lernerbooks.com.

Library of Congress Cataloging-in-Publication Data

Wheeler, Lisa, 1963—
    Dino-boarding / by Lisa Wheeler ; illustrated by Barry Gott.
        pages   cm
    Summary: Meat-eating and vegetarian dinosaurs compete in surfing,
skateboarding, and snowboarding events.
    ISBN 978-1-4677-0213-3 (lib. bdg. : alk. paper)
    ISBN 978-1-4677-0620-5 (EB pdf)
    1. Stories in rhyme. 2. Dinosaurs—Fiction. 3. Extreme sports—Fiction.
4. Competition (Psychology)—Fiction. I. Gott, Barry, illustrator. II. Title.
PZ8.3.W5668Dm 2014
[E]—dc23   2013030724

Manufactured in the United States of America
3-44262-12762-6/15/2017

Loyal fans arrive in hordes
to watch the dinos ride on boards.

Skateboards! Snowboards! Surfboards too!

From park . . . to hills . . . to ocean blue.

Mt. Mastodon has the right conditions

to host the yearly competitions.

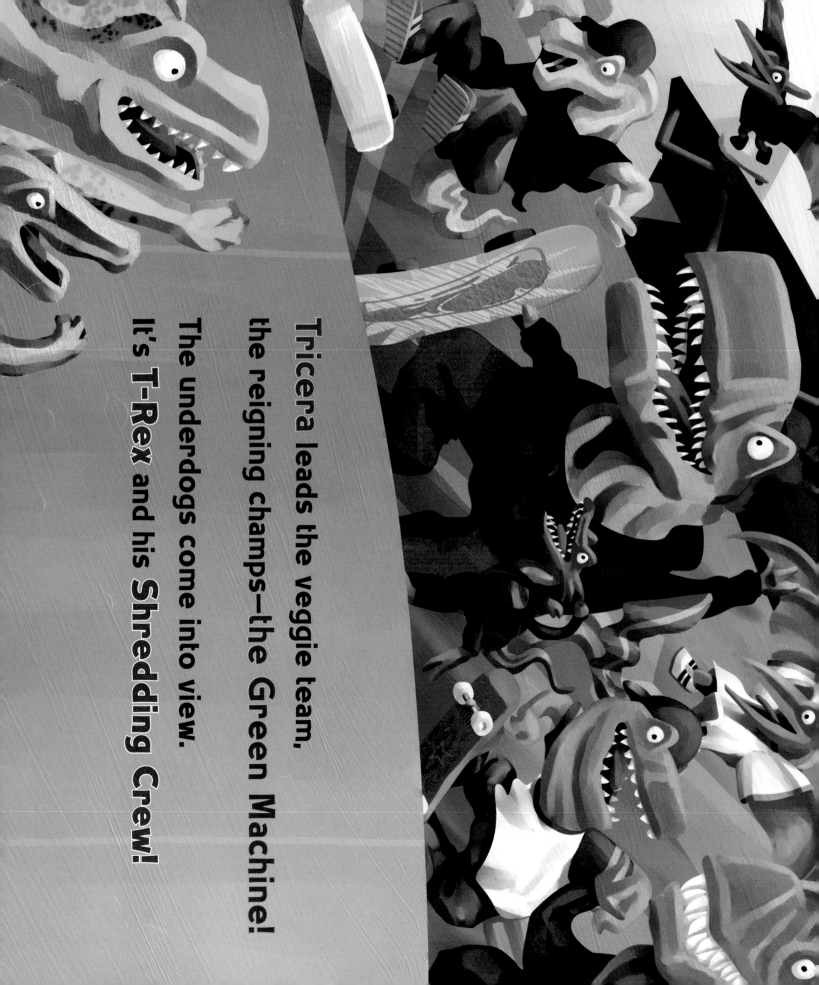

Tricera leads the veggie team,

the reigning champs—the Green Machine!

The underdogs come into view.

It's T-Rex and his **Shredding Crew!**

First, let's take it to the shore
where fans can hear the ocean roar!

Surfboards—both the long and short—
are stars in this aquatic sport.

As bannered planes fly overhead,
Allo represents the red.

Her board is waxed. She's good to go.

She paddles out . . . drops in . . . and *WHOA!*

She gets a big snap off the top,
then snags the barrel, doesn't stop.
She owns the wave! She rides the curl.
Hotdog! That ride was awesome, girl!

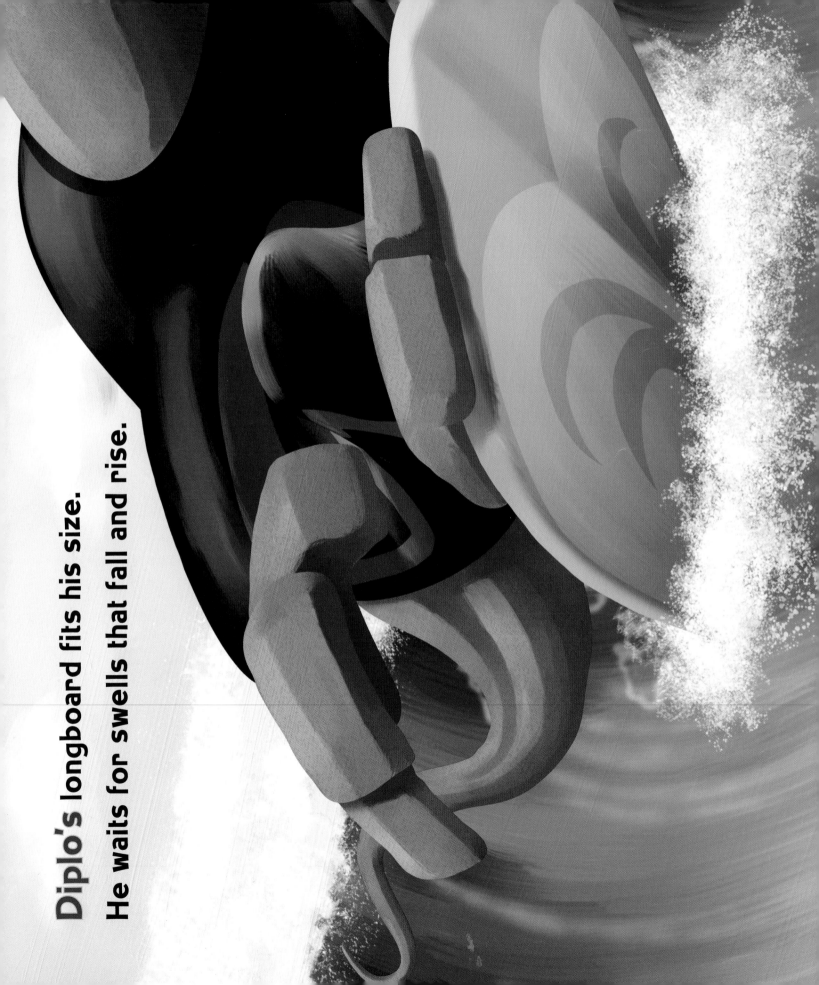

Diplo's longboard fits his size.

He waits for swells that fall and rise.

A monster wave! His ride is sweet—
hangs ten to shore on massive feet.

Compy's a kook—new to this sport.

Is he ready for a board that short?

He doesn't have the moves or skill.

WIPEOUT—yikes!—a gnarly spill.

That perfect wave was much too grand.
Compy should've stayed on land.

Allo earns the highest score!

Surfing's over, but there's more . . .

Time for skateboards! Ready to rock!
More fun begins at one o'clock.

Skateboard launches, ramps and rails,
Dinos padded head to tail.

Long- or shortboards, thin or wide,
graphics on the underside.

Propped on the coping, Raptor grins.
Scans the half-pipe . . .

. . . then drops in!

A blunt to fakie—easy trick.

He needs momentum. Gains it quick.

He goes into a layback air!

It looks like **Raptor's** hanging there.

A few more flips. He nails the landing.

Judges score. The crowd is standing!

He waves to fans and lifts his board.

He came. He saw. He rocked. He scored!

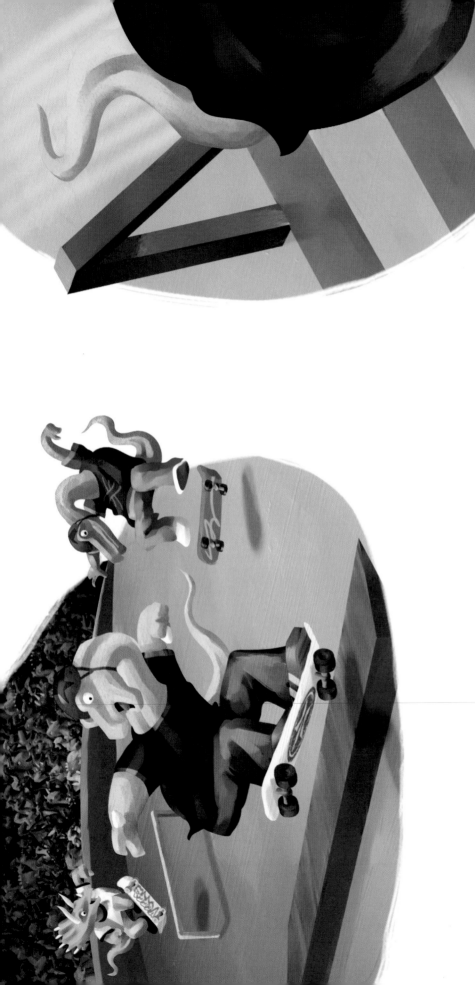

Let's throw some street style into the mix.

This park is equipped for incredible tricks.

Iguano rides goofy—right foot in front.

It took years of practice to master each stunt.

He pops an ollie onto the rail.
Goes for a nose grind—epic fail!
He's too far forward. It's not his day.
Hooray for helmets!

His noggin's okay.

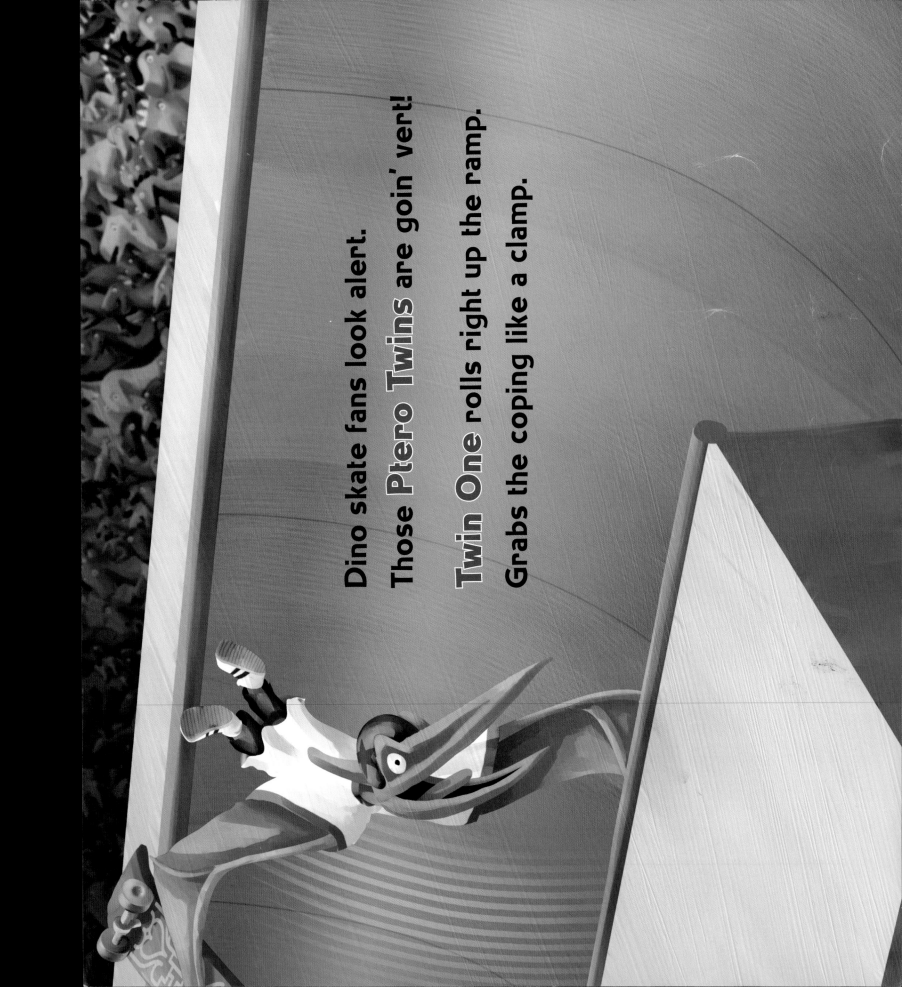

Dino skate fans look alert.

Those Ptero Twins are goin' vert!

Twin One rolls right up the ramp.

Grabs the coping like a clamp.

He's upside down!
But look—his brother!

Ouch!
Those guys slam into each other.

The Green Machine is not amused.

Iguano's still more bashed and bruised.

The **Shredding Crew** enjoys their wins.
But at seven o'clock, Dino-Snowboard begins!

The snowboarders wait at the top of the slope.

Each goggled face is full of hope.

Tricera goes first in the freestyle event.

His clothes hang loose. His knees are bent.

He flies toward the ramp with no hesitation.

A perfect McTwist with a flawless rotation!

He stomps the landing. **Green** fans roar!

Tricera gets a perfect score!

But red fans know their boarder is next.

No shredder is better than awesome T-Rex!

GO T-REX!

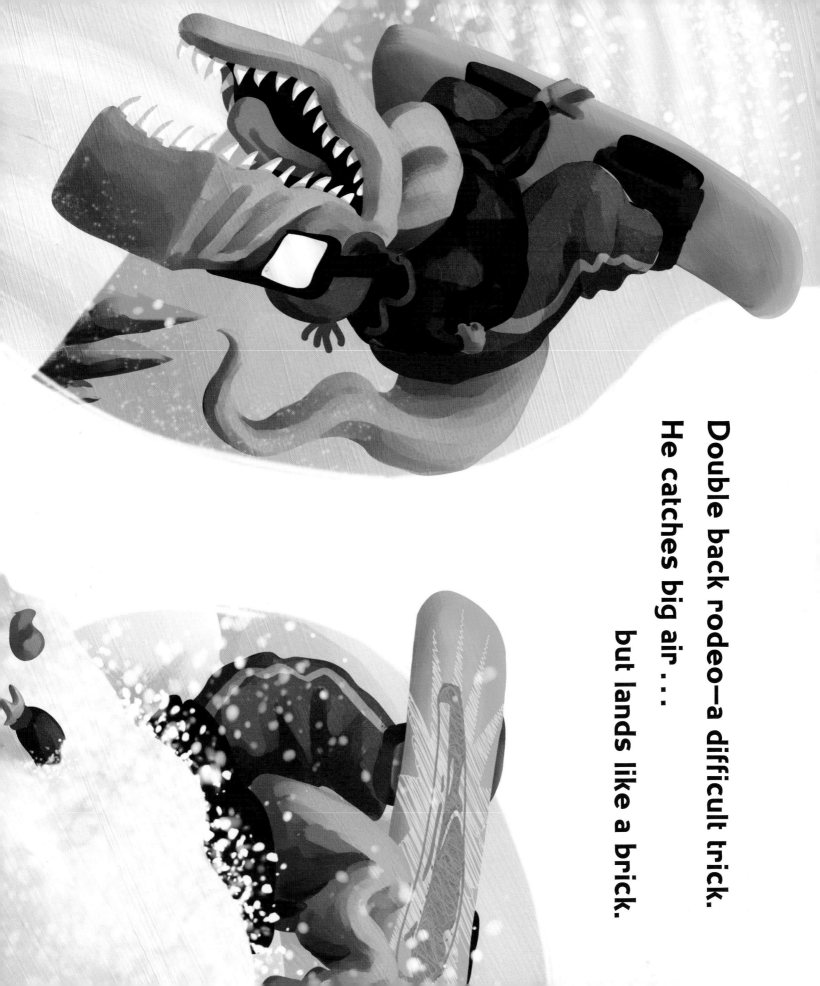

Double back rodeo—a difficult trick.
He catches big air . . .
but lands like a brick.

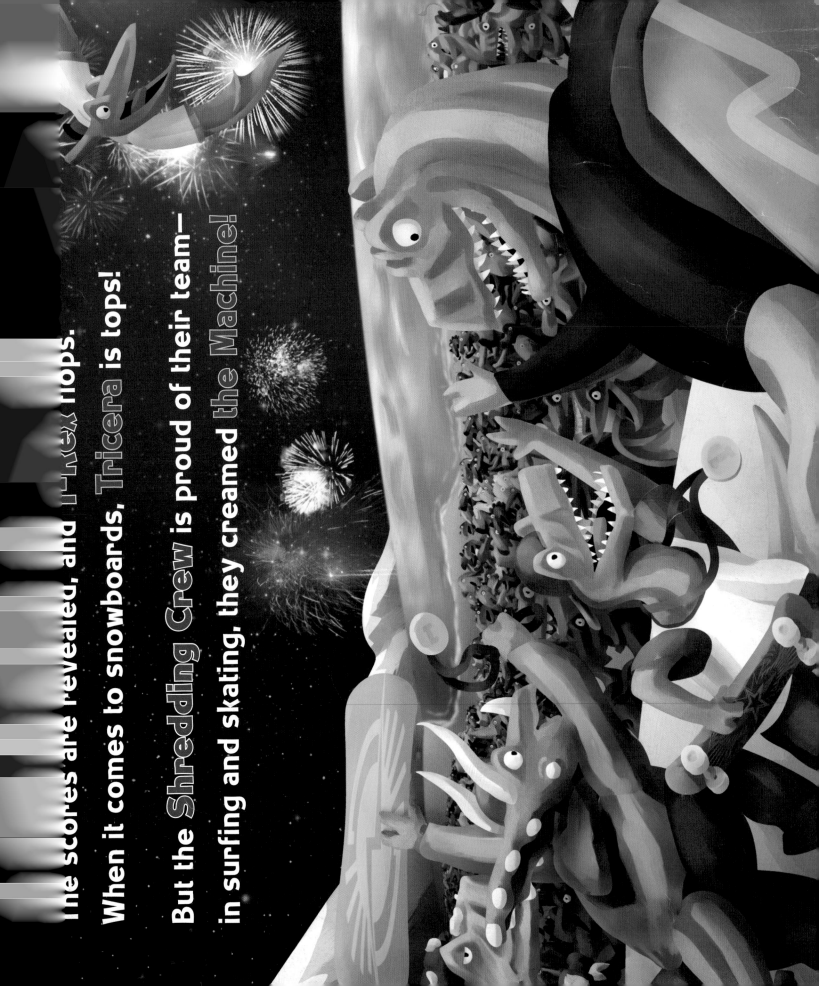

The scores are revealed, and T-Rex flops.

When it comes to snowboards, Tricera is tops!

But the Shredding Crew is proud of their team—

in surfing and skating, they creamed the Machine!

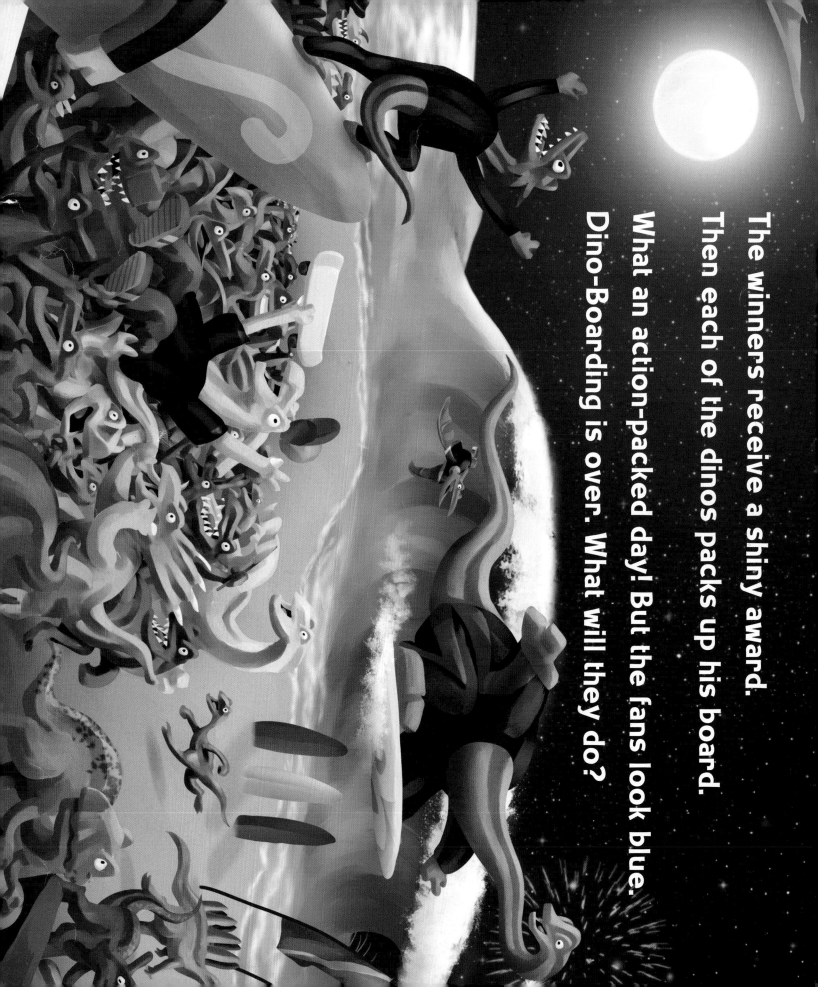

The winners receive a shiny award.

Then each of the dinos packs up his board.

What an action-packed day! But the fans look blue.

Dino-Boarding is over. What will they do?

Fans line up. What's the reason?

Must be Dino-Swimming season!